JBIOG
Monet   Nichols, Catherine
           CLaude Monet

WITHDRAWN

THE
PRIMARY SOURCE LIBRARY
OF
FAMOUS ARTISTS™

CLAUDE MONET

Catherine Nichols

The Rosen Publishing Group's
PowerKids Press™
PRIMARY SOURCE

New York

For Tracy

Published in 2006 by The Rosen Publishing Group, Inc.
29 East 21st Street, New York, NY 10010

First Edition

Editor: Kathy Kuhtz Campbell
Book Design: Emily Muschinske
Photo Researcher: Sherri Liberman

Photo Credits: Cover (left) © Erich Lessing/Art Resource, NY, (right) Private Collection/Bridgeman Art Library/Roger-Viollet, Paris, (background), title page © Christie's Images; p. 4 (top) © Christie's Images/CORBIS, (bottom) © Giraudon/Art Resource, NY; p. 6 (top and inset) Central Saint Martins College of Art and Design, London, UK/Bridgeman Art Library, Musée Marmottan, Paris, France/Bridgeman Art Library, (bottom) Christie's Images, London, UK/Bridgeman Art Library; p. 8 (top) Musée des Beaux-Arts, Rouen, France/Lauros-Giraudon-Bridgeman Art Library, (bottom) © Giraudon/Art Resource, NY; p. 10 (top) © Erich Lessing/Art Resource, NY, (bottom) Bequest of Anne Parrish Titzell/Wadsworth Atheneum, Hartford; p. 12 Kunsthalle, Bremen, Germany/Lauros-Giraudon-Bridgeman Art Library; p. 14 © Archivo Iconografico, S.A./CORBIS; p. 15 © Erich Lessing/Art Resource, NY; p. 16 (top) National Gallery, London, UK/Bridgeman Art Library, (bottom) © Francis G. Mayer/CORBIS; p. 18 (top) © Archivo Iconografico, S.A./CORBIS, (bottom) Musée Marmottan, Paris, France/Giraudon-Bridgeman Art Library; p. 20 Musée d'Orsay, Paris, France/Lauros-Giraudon-Bridgeman Art Library; p. 22 (top) Giverny, Eure, France/Roger-Viollet, Paris/Bridgeman Art Library, (bottom) photos by Sherri Liberman; p. 24 (top) © Giraudon/Bridgeman Art Library, (bottom) Private Collection/Bridgeman Art Library; p. 26 (left) © Burstein Collection/CORBIS, (right) © Alexander Burkatowski/CORBIS; p. 28 (top and bottom) Private Collection/Bridgeman Art Library.

Cover Image: Claude Monet's *Water Lilies*, painted in 1908.

Library of Congress Cataloging-in-Publication Data

Nichols, Catherine.
Claude Monet / Catherine Nichols.— 1st ed.
   p. cm. — (The primary source library of famous artists)
Summary: Discusses the life, work, and legacy of nineteenth-century French Impressionist artist Claude Monet.
Includes bibliographical references and index.
ISBN 1-4042-2761-X (Library Binding)
1. Monet, Claude, 1840–1926—Juvenile literature. 2. Painters—France—Biography—Juvenile literature. [1. Monet, Claude, 1840–1926. 2. Artists. 3. Painting, French.] I. Title. II. Series.
ND553.M7N53 2005
759.4—dc22

2003019149

Contents

Above: *Claude Monet painted* Terrace at Sainte-Adresse *in 1867. Monet's picture shows his father (seated) enjoying a sunny day near the sea, not far from Le Havre. Instead of painting pictures about history and religion, Monet and his artist friends wanted to paint real-life subjects doing everyday activities.*

Left: *Artist Gilbert Alexandre de Severac painted this picture of 25-year-old Claude Monet in 1865.*

A Painter of Light

The French painter Claude Monet is considered one of the most inventive and important artists of his time. Along with his artist friends, including Camille Pissarro and Pierre-Auguste Renoir, he created a new **style** of painting called **Impressionism**. In the 1870s, most French artists followed the rules of the School of Fine Arts in Paris. This school trained artists to paint **classical** and **religious** scenes. It also taught them to make their pictures in **studios**. The students' paintings had to be exact, so that no brushstrokes could be seen. Monet and other Impressionists painted real-life subjects such as railroad stations and trees along the banks of the Seine River. They did not paint using exact brushstrokes. Instead they applied paint in thick, short, broad brushstrokes. They painted outdoors to study the effects of light and color on their subjects. To show a certain moment of light before it changed, they needed to apply dots and dabs of colors to their **canvases** in quick strokes.

Above: In 1860, Monet drew these figures of theater actors so that their features look funny. This type of drawing is called a caricature.
Inset: Honoré Daumier, a popular artist whom Monet respected, drew these caricatures of Frenchmen between 1832 and 1860.

Bottom: Monet painted a storm at sea near Le Havre in 1870.

Growing Up by the Sea

Oscar-Claude Monet was born in Paris, France, on November 14, 1840. His father, Adolphe, was a grocer, a person who sells food and other things. Claude's mother's name was Louise-Justine. Until he was six, he and his family lived in an apartment above the grocery store. In 1845, the Monets moved to Le Havre, in northern France. Jacques Lecadre, Adolphe's brother-in-law, had asked him to join the family's ship **chandler** and grocery business in that harbor town.

Later in life Claude said that as a young boy he had enjoyed walking along Le Havre's beaches and cliffs high above the sea. As he grew older, he liked drawing **caricatures** of teachers and other important people who lived in Le Havre. By age 15, he was selling his funny **portraits** to earn extra pocket money.

Art Smarts

Monet's parents called him "Oscar." Monet signed "Oscar" on his works of art until he was in his early twenties, even though he signed all his letters as "Claude." Monet stopped using the name Oscar in 1862 and used Claude for the rest of his life.

Left: When Monet studied art at the Académie Suisse, he learned how to paint still lifes such as this one, titled Still Life with a Pheasant, *painted in 1861.*

Right: *Eugène Boudin painted this evening scene in Le Havre. Monet went with Boudin on his outdoor painting trips during the late 1850s. Monet said many years later that Boudin once told him, "Do as I do: learn to draw properly and value the sea, the light, the blue sky."*

Becoming a Painter

Monet's mother died when he was 16. The family moved in with Monet's aunt. Through his aunt, Monet met the local painter Eugène Boudin. Boudin painted **landscapes** and **seascapes** and often let Monet go with him when he painted outdoors. Monet decided he wanted to become a painter. His father thought Monet should become a grocer. However, in 1859, he went to study in Paris, which was known for its art schools.

Art Smarts

When Monet went with Boudin to paint outdoors, painting in the open air was unusual. At the time, most artists worked indoors. The invention of tubes of oil paint in the 1840s made it easier for artists to paint outdoors. Before tubes, artists mixed their own oil paints, which were stored in small bags made from the bladders of pigs.

Monet enrolled at the Académie Suisse, a school in which students did not pay for lessons, take tests, or follow exact rules. He learned to draw the human body and **still lifes**. He met other artists and became good friends with Camille Pissarro. Monet also visited the Salon, Paris's most important art **exhibition**, where new artwork was shown yearly.

Top: *Frédéric Bazille painted this picture of his Paris studio in 1870. Monet first met Bazille at their teacher Charles Gleyre's studio in Paris in 1862. Bazille often helped Monet by sharing his studio whenever Monet needed it.*

Bottom: *Pierre-Auguste Renoir made this picture, titled* Monet Painting in His Garden at Argenteuil, *around 1873. Renoir became Monet's friend during their student days at Gleyre's studio.*

The Army and Early Studies

Like all 21-year-old Frenchmen, Monet had to sign up for military service. In 1861, the army sent him to Algeria, a North African country. While serving there, Monet became sick with **typhoid fever**. He returned to Le Havre in August 1862, where he met Dutch painter Johan Barthold Jongkind. Monet liked Jongkind's landscapes and seascapes, which were sunny and showed grand views of the sky.

In 1862, Monet's aunt paid a large sum to free Monet from his army duties. Monet became a student of Charles Gleyre, a well-liked but unadventurous painter in Paris. Gleyre encouraged his students to follow their own artistic interests and suggested improvements in their works. While studying with Gleyre, Monet met three students who, with him and Pissarro, became leaders of the Impressionist movement. They were Pierre-Auguste Renoir, Alfred Sisley, and Frédéric Bazille.

In 1866, instead of finishing Luncheon on the Grass, *Monet painted* The Woman in a Green Dress *for the Salon* exhibition. Monet's girlfriend Camille Doncieux posed for this painting. Sometimes the painting is called Camille. Monet made very large paintings in the 1860s. This one of Doncieux was painted on a canvas that was more than 7 feet (213 cm) high and about 5 feet (152 cm) wide.

Early Paintings

The Salon accepted two of Monet's landscapes for its 1865 exhibition. Art **critics** Pigalle and Paul Mantz praised Monet and his work, calling him a new and original talent. Monet began **excitedly** to work on a painting for the following year's show.

In the summer of 1865, Monet went to the forest of Fontainebleau for the painting's setting. His girlfriend Camille Doncieux and his artist friend Frédéric Bazille posed for him. After completing many drawings, Monet returned to his Paris studio to finish the painting. Monet painted the picnic scene on a canvas that was 15 feet (457 cm) high and 20 feet (610 cm) wide. Monet realized that *Luncheon on the Grass*, as the painting was titled, would not be done in time. It is said that instead he painted *The Woman in a Green Dress* in four days so that it could be in the Salon's 1866 exhibition. This painting was a great success at the Salon show.

The 1866 painting Women in the Garden measured more than 8 feet (244 cm) high and about 7 feet (213 cm) wide. In later years Monet claimed that to paint the work outdoors he had to dig a trench, or long rut in the ground. He used a system of ropes and pulleys to lower or raise the canvas. Pulleys are wheels with grooves so that the ropes can be pulled around them. That way he could work on the upper or lower parts of the painting.

Women in the Garden

Monet never completed *Luncheon on the Grass*. Instead he worked on *Women in the Garden* for the next Salon show. Camille Doncieux posed for all four life-size figures in the picture. When he completed it in the fall of 1866, he sent it to the 1867 Salon judges. They did not choose Monet's painting. However, Frédéric Bazille, who came from a wealthy family, had heard about the painting. He bought *Women in the Garden* for a generous sum.

Monet went back to Le Havre in the summer of 1867 and stayed with his aunt. He could not be away from Doncieux for long, though, because she and Monet were going to have a baby. Monet returned to Paris to be with Doncieux. In August 1867, their son Jean was born. The couple married in June 1870.

Monet painted his and Doncieux's son Jean sleeping in 1868.

Above: The Thames Below Westminster shows London's Houses of Parliament in the distance. Monet painted this picture in 1871, after he and his family had left England and were living in the Netherlands.

Left: Monet made this painting of his floating studio around 1874. He often painted the countryside along the Seine in his floating studio.

Life in London

In 1870, the Monets went to London, England, to escape the **Franco-Prussian War**. Unfortunately Monet's good friend Frédéric Bazille died fighting in the war. Then Monet received word that his father had died. Monet needed to sell paintings to support his family. He met Paul Durand-Ruel, an art dealer from Paris. An art dealer buys and sells artwork. Durand-Ruel had opened a gallery in London and agreed to show Monet's works.

Art Smarts

To paint on the water, Monet had a floating studio built in 1872. He got the idea from painter Charles Daubigny, who went on painting journeys in his boat. Monet's studio boat had a cabinlike building on top of a rowboat so that he could paint inside.

The war ended in May 1871, and the Monets returned to France after a brief time in the Netherlands. They rented a house in Argenteuil, a small town on the Seine River near Paris. These were happy years for Monet. His works were beginning to sell, thanks to the efforts of Durand-Ruel. For the first time, Monet had enough money to live comfortably.

Above: *Monet painted* Impression, Sunrise *in 1872–73. The scene in the painting is the harbor at Le Havre. It was from the title of Monet's painting that he and his friends got the name Impressionists.*

Right: *This is Monet's palette. He mixed the colors of his oil paints on this wooden tray.*

A New Movement

In the early 1870s, Monet and his friends grew tired of having their paintings turned away by the Salon. They decided to hold their own exhibition. In April 1874, they opened their show to the public in the Paris studios of the photographer called Nadar. The exhibition was not successful. Few people showed up, and those who did were not pleased with what they saw. One of Monet's paintings at the show gave the new art movement its name. Critic Louis Leroy saw the show, including Monet's *Impression, Sunrise*. Leroy stated that the artists could produce only "impressions," not finished paintings. In the title of his magazine article, Leroy used "Impressionists," hoping to shame the artists. Later Monet and his friends called themselves Impressionists and their style of art Impressionism.

Art Smarts

From 1874 to 1886 the Impressionists held eight exhibitions. A rich businessman, Ernest Hoschedé, liked Monet's work. In 1876, he asked Monet to paint four pictures for his home near Paris. Monet completed the paintings. However, in 1877, Hoschedé lost all his money and could not pay his bills.

The late 1870s were hard times for Monet and his family. The Monets moved to a less expensive house in Vétheuil, near the Seine River. In the winter of 1878–79, Camille Monet became ill. The Monets had a hard time getting money to buy medicines. Camille died on September 5, 1879. Monet painted Frost near Vétheuil in 1880, after his wife's death.

Sad Times

Once again Monet had money problems. However, he continued to improve his paintings, especially in capturing the play of light on objects. He painted many pictures of the Paris railroad station Saint-Lazare in 1877, making the steam from the trains look real.

Monet's second son, Michel, was born in 1878. The Monets moved to a cheaper house in Vétheuil on the Seine River. They shared the house with Ernest Hoschedé and his family.

In 1879, Monet's wife Camille died after an illness. Monet was heartbroken and could barely paint. When he did, he painted cold, cheerless landscapes such as *Frost near Vétheuil*. He knew he needed to work, so, in 1880, he accepted an invitation to show 18 paintings in a gallery. Critics praised his works.

Art Smarts

Monet painted in all kinds of weather. He became known for his ability to withstand bad weather while painting. During a storm in 1881, he climbed a cliff along a coast in northern France to paint. To keep his easel from falling over, he tied it to a rock. As he painted waves knocked him into the water. He almost drowned.

Top: Monet and his family settled into this house in Giverny in 1883. This photo of the house was taken in 2001. It shows crab apple trees and the main entrance.

Bottom: These photographs show one of the flower beds and some of the flowers in Monet's Giverny gardens. He planted flowers in clumps of different kinds and heights to make the beds look like they were overflowing with flowers. Among them were poppies and irises.

A Home in Giverny

After Monet's one-man exhibition, his paintings sold for high prices. Besides Durand-Ruel, other art dealers sold Monet's works. Monet moved his family to Poissy in 1881. The family now included Alice Hoschedé, who had left her husband, and her children. In 1883, Monet rented a house in Giverny, a small town in northern France. It was to be his last move. He had found a place he loved and he remained there for the rest of his life. He brought his large family, including his two sons, Alice, and her six children.

Monet brought his studio boat to the nearby Epte River for painting trips. As always he painted outdoors for long periods of time. He also reworked or finished paintings in an old barn that he had turned into his studio.

Art Smarts

In Giverny, Monet set about planting a beautiful garden. He planted beds of many colorful flowers. He planted his beds so that they were overflowing and would make the edges of the gravel paths look softer than they really were. He loved his garden and often made paintings of the flower beds.

In 1891, Monet completed his first series of paintings. He chose to paint the haystacks that were in the fields near his Giverny home. He studied the effects of light on the haystacks at different times of the day and in different seasons. Monet painted The Haystacks, or The End of the Summer at Giverny (top) and Haystacks at Sunset, Frosty Weather (bottom) in 1891 as part of this series.

Haystacks and Poplars

In 1888, Monet began to work on a **series** of paintings that dealt with the effects of light on the same objects. The subject of his first series was haystacks. He painted more than 15 paintings of haystacks at different times of day and in different seasons. He tried to show how light at a certain time of day could unify, or connect, objects in a particular view for a moment before the light changed and created a new effect. As the light changed, Monet painted the next effect of the light on a new canvas. Two years later he created a series of paintings of **poplar** trees.

By this time Monet was earning money regularly from his art. He bought the house in Giverny. In May 1891, he showed 15 paintings from the *Haystacks* series. The exhibition, which was titled Recent Works of Claude Monet, was a success. Finally Monet was recognized as an important artist.

Between 1892 and 1894, Monet went to Rouen, France, to paint a series of paintings of the front of Rouen Cathedral. In choosing this subject instead of one from nature, Monet could show the effects of changing light on a solid, unchanging form. The front of the cathedral is seen in the middle of the day (left) and in the morning (above), both painted in 1894.

The Changing Light

Ernest Hoschedé died in 1891. Monet and Alice married the following year. Monet's paintings sold well and visitors flocked to Giverny to see the famous painter.

From 1892 to 1894, Monet painted another series of paintings. His subject this time was not nature but a stone **cathedral** in Rouen, France. Monet rented rooms across the street from the cathedral and painted the cathedral's facade, or front, from the second story of his rooms. He painted 30 paintings in all, showing the building in changing light at different times of the year.

Although Monet loved Giverny and France, he also traveled to distant cities to paint. From 1899 to 1901, he often went to London to paint the Thames River and the Houses of Parliament. He also made trips to Norway, the Netherlands, Italy, and Spain. Wherever he went, he brought with him his easel, paints, and canvases.

Above: *Monet was photographed in his third Giverny studio around 1924. He built this studio in 1915, so that he had a large, sunny space for working. He put the water lily paintings on carts with wheels, called dollies, so that he could roll them next to one another to see what they looked like together. He always planned to have his water lily paintings shown together in one room.*

Right: *Monet is seen here with a friend on the Japanese footbridge that he had built over his pond in 1894.*

A Water Garden

In 1893, Monet bought land near his Giverny house and made a pond. He added a wooden bridge over the pond. He planted **water lilies** and watched them grow. In 1899, he began a series of water lily paintings.

Monet's happiness ended in 1911 when Alice died after being sick. Three years later his son Jean died after an illness. A friend suggested that it might ease Monet's sadness to paint more water lily pictures and give them to the French nation. Monet spent his last years working on these paintings.

Monet's eyesight began to fail. He had **cataracts** and needed eye operations in 1923. When he recovered, he bought eyeglasses and could see clearly again. However, after suffering with a lung illness, Monet died on December 5, 1926, at Giverny, the place he loved most.

Art Smarts

Monet always meant for his huge water lily paintings to be shown together in one place. That way people could see them as a whole. He did not live to see his wish come true. After his death the water lily works were hung in two oval rooms in a Paris museum, the Musée de l'Orangerie.

Timeline

1840	Oscar-Claude Monet is born in Paris, France, on November 14.
1845	Monet moves to Le Havre with his family.
1855	He starts drawing caricatures.
1857	Monet's mother dies.
1859	Monet studies art in Paris.
1861	He enters the army and is sent to Algeria. Monet gets typhoid fever.
1862	Monet studies with Charles Gleyre.
1865	Monet has two paintings accepted at the Salon in Paris.
1867	Monet and Camille Doncieux's son Jean is born.
1870	Monet marries Doncieux. He and his family move to London.
1874	Monet's painting *Impression, Sunrise* gives Impressionism its name.
1878	His second son, Michel, is born.
1879	Monet's wife Camille dies.
1888	Monet starts his painting series *Haystacks*.
1890	Monet buys his home in Giverny.
1892	He marries Alice Hoschedé at the Giverny home.
1899	Monet begins the *Water Lilies* series.
1911	Monet's wife Alice dies.
1926	Monet dies at Giverny on December 5.

Glossary

canvases (KAN-ves-ez) Cloth surfaces that are used for paintings.

caricatures (KAR-ih-keh-churz) Witty pictures of people, with the features of the face made to look larger than they are.

cataracts (KA-teh-rakts) Cloudiness in the lenses of a person's eyes that can cause blindness.

cathedral (kuh-THEE-drul) A large church that is run by a bishop.

chandler (CHAN-ler) A person who supplies a ship with goods for a voyage.

classical (KLA-sih-kul) Concerned with a general study of the arts and sciences.

critics (KRIH-tiks) People who write their opinions about something.

excitedly (ik-SY-ted-lee) In a stirred up way.

exhibition (ek-sih-BIH-shun) A public show of artworks.

Franco-Prussian War (fran-koh-PRUH-shen WOR) The war of 1870–71, fought by France and Prussia, a state that later became Germany.

Impressionism (im-PREH-shuh-nih-zim) A style of painting started in France in the 1860s. Impressionists tried to paint their subjects showing the effects of sunlight on things at different times of day and in different seasons.

landscapes (LAND-skayps) Pictures that show a view of natural scenery.

poplar (PAH-pler) A tall tree that grows rapidly and has wide leaves.

portraits (POR-trets) Pictures, often paintings, of certain people.

religious (ree-LIH-jus) Having to do with a faith, a system of beliefs.

seascapes (SEE-skayps) Pictures that show scenes of the sea.

series (SIR-eez) A group of similar things that come one after another.

still lifes (STIL LYFS) Pictures of nonliving things.

studios (STOO-dee-ohz) Rooms or buildings where artists work.

style (STYL) A certain way in which a work of art is painted or made.

typhoid fever (TY-foyd FEE-ver) An easily caught and often deadly sickness that is usually caused by unclean food and water.

water lilies (WAH-ter LIL-eez) Plants with floating leaves and big flowers that grow in freshwater ponds and lakes.

Index

Primary Sources

Cover. Left. A detail of Claude Monet's *Water Lilies*, painted in 1908, oil on canvas. Monet started his series of water lily paintings in 1899 after he made his water garden and his wooden footbridge, which he modeled on gardens he saw printed in Japanese prints. **Right**. This photograph of Claude Monet in his studio at Giverny was taken by Henri Manuel around 1924. **Page 4. Top**. Monet's *Terrace at Sainte-Adresse* was painted in 1867. Monet's father and aunt are shown near the harbor of Le Havre. Metropolitan Museum of Art, New York. **Page 6. Top**. This caricature, titled *Small Theatrical Pantheon*, was drawn by Monet in 1860. The drawings show some of the popular actors and playwrights of Monet's time. **Inset**. Honoré Daumier made this lithograph of caricatures around 1832–60. Titled *Plate 74.3 Parisian Types "I can tell you are of noble birth.... I have the eye for it"* from *Charivari* magazine, published by Aubert & Co. Central Saint Martins College of Art and Design, London, UK. **Page 10. Top**. Frédéric Bazille completed his work *The Painter's Atelier in the Rue de la Condamine* around 1870, just before he was killed in the Franco-Prussian War. Musée d'Orsay, Paris. **Bottom**. Pierre-Auguste Renoir painted *Monet Painting in His Garden at Argenteuil* around 1875. Wadsworth Atheneum, Hartford, CT. **Page 14**. Monet painted *Women in the Garden* in 1867 for the Paris Salon, but it was rejected. Camille Doncieux posed for all four life-size figures in the painting. Musée d'Orsay, Paris. **Page 15**. Monet painted *Jean Monet Sleeping* in 1868. His son Jean was about one year old. Ny Carlsberg Glyptotek, Copenhagen, Denmark. **Page 16. Top**. *The Thames Below Westminster* was completed by Monet in 1871, after he and his family left London. Monet made many paintings of London and the Thames and returned to the subjects in the 1890s. **Bottom**. *Monet's Studio Boat* was painted by Monet around 1874. Otterlo, Rijksmuseum Kroller-Muller. **Page 18. Top**. *Impression, Sunrise* was painted by Monet in 1872–1873. He showed the painting, which is a harbor scene of Le Havre, in the Impressionists' first exhibition in 1874. Musée Marmottan, Paris. **Bottom**. Monet's palette (wood). The artist used this palette, which is 13 inches by 20 inches (33 x 51 cm). Musée Marmottan, Paris. **Page 22. Top**. Monet's house at Giverny, France. This photograph was taken in 2001. In 1926, Monet's son Michel inherited the house and garden. Michel gave the house to the Academie des Beaux-Arts in 1966. After its restoration in the 1970s, the house has been open to the public since 1980. **Bottom**. These flowers, including allums, poppies, and water lilies, were photographed in the springtime at Giverny by Sherri Liberman. **Page 26. Left**. *Rouen Cathedral, Midday*, was painted by Monet in 1894. Pushkin Museum, Moscow, Russia. **Right**. *Rouen Cathedral Facade and Tour d'Albane (Morning Effect)* was painted by Monet in 1894. Burstein Collection. Photo by Barney Burstein. **Page 28. Top**. Henri Manuel photographed Monet before his water lily paintings in Monet's studio around 1924–25. The paintings behind Monet are the four panels that make up *Morning*, which are now at the Musée de l'Orangerie, Paris.

Web Sites

Due to the changing nature of Internet links, PowerKids Press has developed an online list of Web sites related to the subject of this book. This site is updated regularly. Please use this link to access the list:

www.powerkidslinks.com/psla/monet/